Nevertheless

Sparkian Tales in Bulawayo

Shane Strachan

ISBN 978-0-7974-9257-8
EAN 9780797492578

Published by amaBooks
P.O. Box AC1066, Ascot, Bulawayo
amabooksbyo@gmail.com
www.amabooksbyo.com

Cover Design: Veena Bhana

Illustrations: Duncan Urquhart

Shane Strachan and amaBooks would like to express
their gratitude to Creative Scotland for their support.

ALBA | CHRUTHACHAIL

Shane Strachan lives and writes in the Northeast of Scotland. His work has appeared in *New Writing Scotland, Stand, Gutter* and *Northwords Now* among others, and he has staged theatre work with the National Theatre of Scotland and Paines Plough. He holds a PhD in Creative Writing from the University of Aberdeen and has run creative projects in Scotland, Germany and Zimbabwe. In 2018, he is one of Scottish Book Trust's Robert Louis Stevenson Fellows.

Echoing Muriel Spark's preface to *Aiding and Abetting* – her novel based on the mysterious life of Lord Lucan – I have no doubt that the reality of her time in Africa would 'differ factually and in actual feeling from the story I have told'. What we know of her words, habits and attitudes to people and to life, I have 'absorbed creatively' from her own account of this time in her autobiography *Curriculum Vitae,* as well as the vast archival material at the National Library of Scotland, 'metamorphosing' all of this into the fiction that follows.

These stories have been made possible by Creative Scotland's Endless Different Ways Small Grants Fund which celebrates Spark's centenary in 2018. I would like to thank the staff at the National Library of Scotland (particularly Dr Colin McIlroy), Donald Urquhart who provided the Spark-inspired illustrations, Jane Morris and Brian Jones of amaBooks, and all of the inspiring people I met and travelled with during trips to Bulawayo in 2015 and 2016.

S. S.

Edinburgh, Leith, Portobello, Musselburgh and Dalkeith.

27th August 1937 – South Atlantic Ocean

This was life, what Muriel had been hungry for all those years in Edinburgh. Each day aboard the *Windsor Castle* had been its own little theatre show: new cast members from the six hundred passengers onboard entered her stage to perform monologues about bohemian lives in London, colonial tales from South Africa and gossip about her final destination, Southern Rhodesia. Muriel would recite some of her poems in return and new faces soon sought her out to hear them.

One young South African, Levi Cloote, seemed to have a particular interest in how her lines developed and changed with the passing days. He was twenty, a year older than her, and very tall with fair skin that seemed to cope slightly better in the heat than Muriel's had. When her skin started to peel, she asked Levi to rub cold cream on her red shoulders and he was quick to oblige. As she flicked through her chunky blue copy of *The South and East African Year Book and Guide for 1937*, she enjoyed the sensation of his large hands sliding across her bare skin. They were so much bigger than her fiancé's, more exciting somehow. And Levi's hair was so much thicker and longer than Ossie's short dark curls. But for all she knew, Levi could go bald by the time he was the same age as Ossie in a decade's time and the South African sun might dry his skin and age him rapidly, like some of the other Afrikaners aboard the ship, like his parents. She supposed his father was still handsome – even he had a twinkle in his eye for

Muriel – so she turned over in the deckchair, looked up into Levi's eyes and invited him to kiss her.

The next day, the *Windsor Castle* began crossing the tumultuous Bay of Biscay and most of the passengers were quickly bedded with seasickness. With blurred vision and an aching stomach, Muriel resigned herself to lying in her third-class cabin, a level below Levi and his family, while the ship rocked wildly. As she was tossed around in her bunk, she began to wonder if she'd ever make it to Africa alive; she was so violently sick she started to wish for it all to be over, whatever way God willed.

The seas finally calmed and once Muriel was able to walk in a straight line and keep a meal down, young lust and the summer heat soon had her and Levi fired up again. Each night, matters between them progressed in the natural manner but only after they'd spent the day playing deck games, dancing to impromptu bands in the lowest cabin, and chatting in the dark while spotting pockets of dazzling blue phosphorescence in the sea below and constellations of twinkling stars in the Milky Way above.

Now, as the ship approached land and the flat brown peak of Table Mountain spread across the skyline, Muriel knew that her love affair had to come to an end. Levi's parents had suggested that she might rather stay in Cape Town and maybe one day marry their son, but while Levi was rather pleasing to the eye, it was a Mind she wished to marry, and Levi had proved of little use in discussing her poetry in the end, or in discussing anything of importance for that matter. Her Ossie was different. Yes, he'd been a little reserved when they'd first met at the dances in Edinburgh, a little moody and mysterious. And he wasn't the best to look at... But he was smart, a teacher. He had a Mind. And was she not loyal, to some extent?

Besides, she couldn't quite bear the thought of changing her name from Muriel Camberg to Muriel Cloote. She wouldn't be able to set foot in Scotland ever again for them calling her Clootie Dumpling. No no. Ossie's surname would be a much better fit.

She took her engagement ring out of her purse and put it back on her ring finger. Its wee diamond sparkled in the African sun. She smiled at the thought that she might sparkle here too.

15th November 2016 – Bulawayo, Zimbabwe

After struggling to sleep since leaving Aberdeen, Margaret and I find enough energy to chat on the final short flight from Jo'burg to Bulawayo as the sun rises and lights up the orange plains below us where South Africa, Botswana and Zimbabwe meet.

So do you live in Rosemount by yourself Duncan? Margaret asks. She works with me at the maternity hospital in Aberdeen as a Consultant Obstetrician and Gynaecologist. She's around fifteen years older than me, a widow and the mother of three boys. Her job, husband's passing and children are evident in the dark bags under her eyes.

Eh, I do now. Live by myself. I'm not long out of a relationship, I reply.

Oh right. Well I hope it was all… amicable.

Yeah, he's still a friend. He's a good guy.

Margaret glances over at the Zimbabwean couple in the aisle across from us. They both have headphones on. She turns back to me.

That's nice, she whispers.

In the silence that follows, I look back out the window. Bulawayo's airport comes into view. It's not unlike Aberdeen's: a long rectangular structure that looks like a giant metal shed. I feel my stomach sink as the plane descends towards the tarmac. It lands with a thud and a screech.

The arrivals hall is a lot cooler than outside and it's quiet. We don't feel the need to rush as we fill in our visa forms and count out the $55 fee from our bags. Everything at the immigration counter is recorded on paper by solemn-faced Zimbabwean men in glass boxes. It takes an age for each person in the queue to answer the questions and have their passports stickered and stamped.

Your date of birth? my server asks me.

Third of April, nineteen eighty-eight.

Business or tourism?

Business I guess.

What business?

I'm a doctor. I turn and point at Margaret who is picking a loose strand of black hair off her linen suit jacket. We're both doctors. We're visiting the maternity hospital at UBH. Lady Rodwell.

How long?

Just four nights.

The man flicks back through my passport, rereads my form, stares up at me, looks back again at my photograph and then finally reaches for his stamp. When he hands my passport back through the small opening in the glass, I can feel sweat beading on my brow and a tightness in my chest. I make my way through the gate and stand with the handful of other arrivals waiting for the hold luggage. Two men in oil-smeared hi-vis vests cart a trolley of luggage into the hall and swiftly begin dragging the cases off, placing them in rows at random. I grab my case and Margaret's before she makes it through immigration, but we end up having to wait for our box of medical training equipment at the very bottom of the pile.

Before we get a chance to take it, a stout woman insists that we have the box checked by her large x-ray machine. We oblige.

My mouth feels dry and clammy as I explain to her what she's seeing on the screen.

They're just some dolls and some models of the human pelvis, I say before pointing at my hips. I quickly realise it looks more like I'm pointing at my crotch.

They're made of plastic. They're just for demonstration.

She makes us open the box anyway to show her what's inside. The remaining arrivals watch along with the staff as I pull a baby doll out from the box. The stout woman yelps, but quickly realises that its sleepy-eyed expression and gaping mouth are permanent features. Her eyes widen when Margaret pulls out one of the pelvises, but Margaret is quick to encourage her to stroke the plastic model with her hand. I decide not to pull out any of the mock placentas.

Thankfully the woman lets us box everything up and continue on our way out of the arrivals hall, but we're stopped once again at the exit by two Zimbabwean men dressed in creased shirts and baggy black trousers.

The purpose of your visit?

We explain all over again about being doctors. Lady Rodwell. The training. They don't take any notes but simply glance at each other and then stare back at us.

Where are you staying?

The Holiday Inn. By the hospital.

Hmm.

I'm sorry, Margaret bursts. But we really must be getting on. Our flight was delayed and one of the doctors should hopefully still be waiting outside the airport for us.

Oh, I am very sorry, madam doctor, one of the men says in a high-pitched whine. The other stifles a laugh. Enjoy your stay.

We make our way through to the main exit of the airport. Margaret wheels her suitcase behind her as I push my case and the box of training equipment on a broken trolley that keeps veering to the left.

That was a bit hairy.

Yes, Margaret replies. We'll have to watch what we say. And you might...

Might what?

You might want to avoid mentioning your private life.

Private life?

Yes. It's illegal here. It shouldn't have to be that way. But it's their law. Just be careful. Be respectful.

Respectful?

Margaret sighs.

You know what I mean. It's Africa.

Not all of Africa–

Well, we're here as medical professionals, not human rights campaigners. We're only here five days. Let's just make things as easy as possible and have a nice time, eh?

Sure.

I feel my cheeks burning. I wish I hadn't said anything about my ex to her, but at the same time, it's because of James and his frustrations with me being in the closet that had made me vow to be more open about being gay. If I had just been more comfortable with myself in the first place he might have stayed, and I wouldn't have broken down at work and been first choice to go on this random trip to get me out the hospital for a few days. And they'd sent me to *this*: a closet the size of a continent.

Dr Sibanda is standing in the shade outside the entrance, fanning her face with a newspaper. She looks plumper than when we first spoke over Skype last month; her black skirt and white blouse are tightfitting.

Sorry we're late. We got delayed by half an hour, Margaret says as she shakes Dr Sibanda's hand.

No worries. No rush. I needed a break from the hospital, Dr Sibanda says before giggling. Oh! she exclaims turning to me to shake my hand. You are more handsome in real life! So handsome.

I smile and blush.

Nice to meet you properly, Dr Sibanda, I say as we walk over to her small red Mazda, one of only three cars in the parking lot.

Call me Sisa. We're friends now.

Once we're on the road, Sisa and Margaret chat in the front about what it's like to work in a maternity hospital in Scotland. I look out the window as we turn onto Robert Mugabe Way: the city before us slowly builds up from small tin-roof houses to sports fields and business complexes. The wide roads populate with lots of nippy wee cars and minibuses packed full of people crammed on top of one another.

I spot a pile of old newspapers in the back seat next to me. I sift through them and read the headlines at random:

Man stabs wife to death in WhatsApp message row

Cop 'rapes' Grade 7 pupil

Booze binge kills MSU student

5

Ndolwane tackles child brides

President's speech corrected
5

Circumcision to aid conception kills Binga woman

I can't help but read the start of the last article:

A 33-YEAR-OLD woman from Binga, who was desperate to conceive, died after bleeding for more than a week following a botched circumcision during which her husband's grandmother cut off parts of her genitalia.

I feel queasy from a mixture of what I've read, carsickness and the heat. Sisa's air conditioning isn't working, so I open the window a little and let the breeze cool my face. We're now in the centre of town where beautiful jacarandas line either side of the street; their lilac petals flutter down onto the car and slip in through the opening in the window.

Sisa points ahead to a statue of a national hero, but I'm too distracted by long winding lines of people outside various grand buildings.

What are all the queues for?

Sisa sighs.

The government are introducing bond notes. Everybody wants their U.S. dollars out of the banks. The banks only let customers withdraw a little a day. It's been like this for weeks.

Bond notes? I ask.

Yes. Fake money. Pretend dollars. No one wants fake money.

Why are they doing that? Margaret says, shaking her head.

All the dollars are leaving the country. Too many imports, not enough exports. They need something to–

Plug the gap? Margaret says. God.

People are scared. We can't go through hyperinflation again. Those were the worst years. The sooner… that man goes, the better. We hope and pray. That's all we can do.

I look back down at the old newspapers next to me and at the photograph below the headline 'President's speech corrected'. The man in the picture looks old and frail, yet coldly determined.

We drive on past the Holiday Inn after Margaret makes the decision to head straight to the hospital since the Director is expecting us and we're already behind schedule. Sisa turns onto the United

Bulawayo Hospitals driveway and we slowly curve towards the group of white buildings. I realise how tired and dehydrated I am and how much of a struggle it'll be to put on a face, but I'm still grateful to be here and to get away from Aberdeen for a few days.

We park near an outside waiting area where tired-looking families sit in the limited shade of a pop-up gazebo and some bare trees. I take a deep breath before I make my way out of the car to follow behind Sisa and Margaret. Under the low morning sun, our long shadows cross the gravelly car park towards Lady Rodwell Maternity Hospital.

7 July 1938 – Bulawayo, Southern Rhodesia

The Ford V8 rattled along the two uneven strips of tar as they headed east of the town centre toward Lady Rodwell Nursing Home. Whenever Muriel's neighbour Peter failed to align the wheels with the tar, orange dust erupted into the air and clouded the only window she could see through from the back as she lay across the hot, sticky leather seat. She rested her heavy head on Cacile's lap and spread her bent legs wide in an attempt to ease the immense pressure building between them. She tightly gripped Cacile's spindly black hand with her swollen white one as she recited a ballad with the remaining energy she could muster. She'd learnt it as a child and hoped she would live to teach it to the child within her that seemed intent on snapping her lower spine.

O wha will shoe my bonny foot?
  And wha will glove my hand?
And wha will lace my middle jimp
  Wi a lang, lang linen band?

O wha will kame my yellow hair
  With a new made silver kame?
And wha will father my young son,
  Till Lord Gregory come hame?

Oh, Mrs Spark, Cacile kept whispering as she ran her fingers through Muriel's hair with her free hand. Oh, Mrs Spark.

The car abruptly halted and Cacile had to reach out and hold onto Muriel's side to stop her tipping off the seat. Peter opened the door from outside and then stood a moment as though checking that Muriel hadn't stained his precious car with her blood. She reached out a hand and he eventually did the same. He pulled her towards him as she slid herself across the seat with Cacile propping her up from behind.

Now, open the door, Lord Gregory,
   Open the door, I pray!
For thy young son is in my arms,
   And will be dead ere day.

Once she was up on her bare swollen feet, Muriel took a hold of Peter and Cacile's elbows and they slowly walked with her up towards the stoep outside Lady Rodwell. A new mother sat in a wicker chair, cradling her sleeping baby in the evening light. She got up and called inside and a young nurse soon ran out of the entrance, papers in hand. The nurse addressed Muriel only. Her hand sped across the page as she noted down the clipped answers Muriel gave in between her ballad verses.

Peter headed back to his car, mumbling something about going to find Mr Spark. The car soon spluttered and grumbled away from the hospital.

Once the nurse was finished with her notes, she took Muriel's free arm and then glared at Cacile who quickly let go of Muriel and stepped back, her head hung low.

Thank you, Muriel gasped at Cacile. She tried to smile but instead let out a moan as pain surged through her. Cacile slowly turned and began walking back along one of the strips of tarmac.

The dark parquet flooring cooled and soothed the soles of Muriel's feet as she shuffled down the dim corridor with the nurse. In black capital letters a handwritten sign read DELIVERY ROOM above an open door on their right. She glimpsed in. Even though she was quick to turn away again, she could not unsee the pool of bright red blood on the tiled floor that a young nurse was mopping up.

As she was shown into one of the labour wards on the left, she continued to recite the ballad quietly, relieved to have come upon a lull between contractions.

> *The wind blew loud, the sea grew rough,*
> *And dashed the boat on shore.*
> *Fair Annie floated through the faem,*
> *But the baby raise no more.*

She supposed it was because she missed the sea that this particular ballad had come to mind. Its morbid nature did not perturb her; she'd been brought up on the stuff. The two other women in the ward didn't seem as keen as she finished the recital: *She turned fair Annie frae my door, wha died for love o me*.

She lay down on her back and clenched her eyes tight to block out their hard, sweaty faces; to block out the sight of the prison-like bed she'd been subjected to, a thin mattress sat atop a chunky metal frame; to block out the sickly orange light streaming in from the veranda at the other end of the room. She longed for darkness.

The contractions started up again, this time like electric shocks jolting across her belly and back. Beads of sweat and tears slid across her temples down onto the lumpy pillow. She wished her friend Tootsie Bailey were here by her bedside to hold her hand as she did on their private sunrise walks round Central Park where Muriel would tell of her life back in Scotland and Tootsie would do the same of England.

If only Cacile were allowed to enter the hospital and keep her company. She would be walking back now to her home in the west of Bulawayo: the natives' side. To think that Muriel had travelled all this way to escape those dull schisms between Edinburgh's Old and New Towns, between rich and poor, the have and have-nots, and instead of adventuring upon a different way of being as she'd hoped, she'd only come upon more divides: White – Black – Coloured; British – Dutch – Native; rich whites – poor whites; the many men – the few women; and worst of all, husband and wife. She wept just as much over that as she did at the unrelenting pain that continued to course through the very core of her, worsening in frequency as the light from the veranda disappeared with the setting of the sun.

Through the night, she didn't get a second of sleep for the contractions and the noises of the other two women on the ward; they were never the three of them in chorus, but seemed to each take up a verse, one after the other. To deal with her own pain, Muriel chewed at her nails until one began bleeding and left little dark specks where she clenched her pillow and sheet.

When the sun rose, Muriel was certain that her husband Ossie had appeared at one point in the middle of the night to see her. She knew for sure when he returned to the hospital that evening bearing two gifts in his small hands: a manicure set to fix her nails and a bouquet of lilies he'd picked up in town. After being in labour for almost a day, she could have flung the manicure set at him. And the flowers... she'd fallen for such a performance in the past, once upon a sickbed in Edinburgh when he'd come calling to her family's flat on Bruntsfield Place with a fistful of bluebells. He'd told her of his teaching contract in Africa, how he'd like her to join him, how lonely he'd be without her. He'd known that the bluebells would match the cushions in her room, made from one of her English grandmother's old dresses that was so special to her. And then there were the pink and yellow gerbera daisies she'd been gifted by the Thomas Cook rep when she'd stepped off the boat in Cape Town; they'd wilted so quickly in the heat. She'd learnt to see these bouquets as harbingers of the variety of distresses to come, each flower a different drama yet to unfold.

You were right, she said to Ossie in between deep breaths. I shouldn't have gone through with this. I don't think we can do this.

Magnified by his spectacles, she caught his eyes darting over at the other women in the room. He sighed and ran his fingers through his short curly hair.

Aren't you going to say something? she seethed through gritted teeth.

He turned from her and ran a finger along the bedside table. He inspected the grey dust that had accumulated on his fingertip. He often did this in their boarding house, marching from room to room until he finally came upon an undusted surface to bollock at Cacile about cleaning.

For a new building, this place is filthy, he sneered. You'd think it was a hospital for the natives.

Muriel turned away from him and sobbed into her pillow as her belly seared and throbbed with pain once more. She was going to die in childbirth, she was sure of it. Die at the age of twenty in the middle of this godforsaken land thousands of miles from home. She pulled the thin bed sheet up over her head and hid herself away from the watching eyes of the labour ward.

It was the next afternoon that the baby boy arrived just as Muriel thought she would finally expire from exhaustion. When she eventually came round from a deep sleep the day after, Ossie argued with her about giving the child the same middle name as himself. With what little fight she had left, Muriel ensured that her son did not have the same cursed initials as his father Sidney Oswald Spark. They agreed to name the boy Samuel Robin, but she soon found herself referring to him as her Sonny.

Ossie departed from Lady Rodwell to wire their parents with the news. Avoiding eye contact with the other new mothers in the postnatal ward, Muriel gently lifted the baby from his cot and headed out onto the first-floor veranda. Its red tiles were hot against the bare soles of her feet; she was quick to sit down in the wicker armchair and let her feet swing and cool in the air as she squinted at the dazzling orange wasteland stretching away from Bulawayo. Sonny began crying and so she rocked him in her arms. His wee face wasn't quite human in feature yet, but rather pointed and alien-like.

Quietly, she sang a song to the bairn and thought of her own mother back in Edinburgh who sang it at the piano on long summer nights.

Rose in the bud, the June air's warm and tender,
Why do you shrink your petals to display?
Are you afraid to bloom in crimson splendour,
Lest someone come and steal your heart away?

Rose in the bud, the evening sun is sinking,
Wait not too long and trifle with fate.
Life is so short and love is all, I'm thinking,
Love comes but once, and then, perhaps, too late.

At least the birth would bring cheer to her parents. She couldn't help but weep at this thought of home.

The baby eventually fell asleep and they both turned quiet. She could hear the call of a grey lourie somewhere in the distance. Its *kweh*-ing unavoidably morphed into those words Muriel couldn't help but imagine were a command specifically for her: *go-away... go-away... go-away...*

18th November 2016 – Bulawayo, Zimbabwe

After three days at Lady Rodwell, I will never complain about the NHS again. As well as all my moping over James leaving me, I've started to wonder if that's why I was selected to go on the trip: I whine about the job. I complain everyday. I somehow think I have a rougher deal than everyone else – the longest shifts, the most awkward patients. But I've come to realise over the past few days at Lady Rodwell that I don't have to deal with trying not to trip over missing blocks of parquet flooring every time I enter my work. I don't have to grip the bannister tight when I go up the stairs because the lift's been broken for over a year and the middle of each step is missing due to oxygen tanks having to be dragged up two flights of stairs to keep premature babies on the top floor alive. I don't have to spend my own wages paying for my patient to have a much-needed caesarean section so she and her baby can live.

Of course, in a few months' time, all of this will probably be a distant memory and my petty grievances will once again seem important in relation to the ease of life I was born into. I will moan and I will complain and I will falsely think I am hard done by all over again. But for now I'm still in a state of shock and trying not to fall asleep from the exhaustion of it all in the back of Sisa's car.

Under an overcast sky, we're heading south of the city to the wilds of the Matopos, a thank you from the hospital for sharing our 'expertise', something I feel I gave very little of. I could barely get a word in edgeways for Margaret's impromptu lectures from which, I'm pretty sure, the staff and medical students learned nothing new. We'd been as well just mailing the equipment over.

Before we reach Matobo National Park we're stopped by two different police roadblocks. At the first, a policewoman asks to check Sisa's radio licence, even though she never listens to the radio because it's government controlled. Her papers are in order and so they let us head onwards. At the second roadblock, the policeman insists that Sisa tests all of her lights for him. She complies, even though it's the middle of the day and the lights will barely be visible. The policeman returns to the car and hands Sisa a fine as one of her indicator lights isn't working.

Which one? she asks in English rather than Ndebele so we know what's going on.

Thirty dollars, the policeman says.

Which light is broken? Left or right?

Twenty dollars, the policeman says.

Left or right?

Ten dollars.

Sisa opens the glove compartment and takes out her purse. She hands a dirty crumpled note over to the policeman. He takes it from her and grins a gap-toothed smile before skipping back over to the other four officers milling around at the side of the road.

At the park entrance, Margaret insists on paying the fee for all of us and we're soon heading through the gate and along the bumpy orange dirt track. At first, the landscape doesn't quite look the same as did it in the pictures I googled last night. There's hardly a hint of green. The trees are almost bare and there are little black stumps where thatches of grass surely must have stood.

Ah… Sisa says. More fires.

Because it's so dry? Margaret asks.

Yes. The dryness. Sometimes people.

In amongst the bleached-out landscape I spot some movement. I ask Sisa to stop and I point to where I'm sure I saw something disrupt the great stillness.

Warthogs, Sisa whispers.

The two beasts come closer to us. They are nothing like the warthogs I've seen on TV. They are emaciated to the point they look like miniature grey horses. They move slugglishly, sniffing around the different remains of charred bush.

We drive on, but it takes a good five minutes or so to get beyond the scorched land and reach something greener. We come to a valley where columns of round golden rocks are stacked high up on the hills. I can't help but continually scan the landscape for signs of wildlife, but the skies are clearing and it's beginning to get much hotter so I start to doubt we'll see much now.

Sisa parks by the side of one of the hills and asks us to follow her up the steps nearby. She has to keep stopping to catch her breath. Margaret and I wait for her and take time to appreciate the view from a higher perspective. At the top, Sisa takes an inhaler out of her handbag.

Asthma? I say, asking the obvious.

Yes, Sisa wheezes. A lot of people I know have it. I think it's the jacarandas. The pollen.

Hmm.

Once she's recovered, Sisa guides us over to a wired-off crevice in the rock. I spot a couple of wasps lazily float through the wire and I fear it's caged off because there are nests inside.

Cave paintings, Margaret gasps.

I squint at the wall in front of her and my eyes slowly adjust to make out a row of red figures leaping through the air with bows and arrows in hand. After I take a couple of pictures on my phone, I realise that fainter still among the human figures are outlines of wildebeests and giraffes, and further along the yellow-grey rock, a large rhino is depicted. The paintings are so alive for something so ancient. It makes me itch to see some of these animals for real.

As we head back down to the car, I spot tiny holes in the ground where termites or some other bugs have been burrowing. I take a couple of pictures and Sisa laughs at me.

It is funny that you notice this, that you want to take a picture. She giggles again. I am thinking, why would he take a picture of *this*? Of the ground?

I shrug my shoulders and laugh with her.

Further along the road, Sisa asks us if we want to visit the gravesite of Cecil John Rhodes.

That might be interesting, Margaret begins.

I'd rather try to see some animals if that's okay? I say quickly, like ripping off a plaster.

Margaret glances round at me and smiles awkwardly.

Well, I suppose I've seen enough gravestones in my time, she mumbles.

We continue on along the track and enjoy pointing out all the different rock formations. Sisa explains that Matopos means 'bald heads' in Ndebele, and all I can see from then on in these stacks of golden granite boulders are figures rising up out of the bush.

The skies are completely clear by the time we stop for a late lunch by Maleme Dam and the heat starts to beat down. Three monkeys clamber up rocks in the distance as we eat through supermarket sandwiches we picked this morning. They are unpleasantly warm.

Let's hope the rain falls soon, Sisa says as we look out onto the near empty dam.

Sisa and I decide to take a walk around it while Margaret gives her sons a call to check up on them since they'll be home from secondary school back in Scotland.

At the very edge of the dam there is a paddling pool's worth of stagnant, swampy water. Now and then, dark-brown bubbles rise up to the surface and fish thrash around. We can only watch this torture for so long before we have to turn back.

Sisa tells me that she is expecting a third child and I congratulate her.

Do you have kids? she asks.

No.

But you're married?

No.

But you're twenty-eight. And a doctor!

I try to smile.

Well… people don't tend to settle down until a bit later in Scotland.

Sisa laughs and exposes all of her brilliantly white teeth.

2

If you were African, you'd have been married a long time ago. Especially a handsome doctor like you. Ha!

My pace quickens back towards Margaret. I feel hot and my heart thumps in my chest.

Even though I can tell Margaret is ready to leave when we get back into the car, I agree to Sisa taking us to another dam in the hope we might see some more animals.

When we arrive at the next dam, Mpopoma, there is far more water and I'm hopeful. We sit for half an hour chatting about Lady Rodwell's abundance of broken equipment. Sisa explains most of it has been donated from NGOs in years past only to break soon after with no parts available anywhere nearby and no offer of replacements from the NGOs. The direness of it all soon subdues us to silence.

Just as Margaret begins to suggest we head back, I finally spot some movement in the water.

Is it a hippo?

Sisa sighs.

It's a crocodile.

A crocodile. Wow, Margaret says flatly.

My friend Harrison, he works for the park. He told me about this crocodile. They think a… European came and put it here. Someone whose pet got a little too big. Too dangerous.

You're joking? I say.

I wish, Sisa laughs. I wish.

Margaret points out the time and Sisa panics realising we only have twenty minutes to make it back through the park gates before they're locked.

As we speed back along the track and the sun starts to set, we begin to see some of the animals I'd been searching for all day. There is a pair of wildebeests in the distance, meandering across the grassland; a giraffe peers round at us in between plucking leaves from the top of a high tree; and three zebras gallop away from the sound of Sisa's speeding Mazda. At first, I try to capture pictures of them all on my phone, but I fail to get anything other than a blur and I become frustrated. I realise this frustration comes from the fact that I've been taking all of these pictures so I can post them on Instagram. I want James to see that I'm doing something exciting and different with my life now. To see that I've travelled to a far away place. That I can be fun and adventurous. That I can be the things he left me for to try and find in someone else.

I decide to put my phone away and watch the zebras gallop through the bush for myself. Their stripes merge into one zigzagged blur before they break apart to roam free on their own. The dry earth rises in the air behind them in billowing golden clouds.

***14th November 1941 – Bulawayo, Southern
Rhodesia***

It was always something of a relief for Muriel to
slowly open her eyes each morning and see that the

wall above her head was not puckered with bullet holes. She sat up and realised she'd fallen asleep amongst her books and papers again. The last thing she'd scribbled down in her notebook was a line from one of Kierkegaard's journals: *Not until a man has inwardly understood himself and then sees the course he is to take does his life gain peace and meaning.*

She looked over at Sonny's bed. His nanny, Esther, must have come in at some point and taken him away. Muriel was thankful to not have been woken by either of them. She'd stayed up quite late reading and she'd been invited to a dance tonight at the Grand Hotel. She would need to reserve her energy for that.

Esther really had been an angel to her and Sonny since Muriel had finally decided to separate from Ossie and make the move from Gwelo back to Bulawayo. She often wondered if Esther's devotion to them was fuelled by the fact Muriel clearly didn't give a damn that she was coloured; it seemed to bother just about everyone else, including Esther's white father over in Durban. Like she'd done years before with her friend Tootsie, Muriel would go for long morning walks in Central Park with Esther as they talked about the lives they'd led as outcasts and outsiders; over time Esther's English had become flavoured with a hint of Muriel's Scottish accent.

There was a knock. May's beautiful ash-blonde hair slowly appeared round the side of the door. Like Muriel, May had reluctantly found herself having to raise a child on her own as her husband had gone off to fight in the war. There was no passage home available to the women and strictly none for their children. Living together had seemed the best way to make the most of what little resources they had – mainly Esther and May's chef Moses – in order to endure this life so distant and so different from home.

Sorry to bother you but Esther tells me that Moses is sick this morning, May said with a slight waiver to her voice. We'll have to prepare breakfast ourselves. Can you come and help me?

I couldn't possibly. It's imperative I finish this volume before I head to work. I'll lose the thread of it if I leave it until after this weekend. And besides, I've never prepared a breakfast in my life. Can't Esther do it?

Her hands are rather full looking after Sonny and Gail.

Knowing May's eyes would follow hers, Muriel sighed and stared over at her Rhodesian Eisteddfod award certificates pinned up on the wall opposite her bed: the first was for a poetry win in the spring of 1939. The second was a prose award from the summer just past.

Very well, May said quietly. I'm sure I'll manage on my own.

Thank you. Oh, and I'll have a cup of tea if you're boiling the kettle.

May sniffed a laugh before making her way back out of the room. She was one for the books herself – a Classics scholar – but she seemed not to be as devoted to reading as Muriel. It was as though having a degree had proved her capabilities as a thinker and she no longer felt as eager to participate in the engagement of the Mind. Muriel had no university degree and felt her award certificates were the only validation she had to pursue her studies.

An hour later, having completed her reading in the bath, dressed for work and eaten May's rather underwhelming attempt at breakfast, Muriel gave Sonny a kiss goodbye on his wee head and handed him his stuffed bunny. Today he looked a little more like her father and a little less like Ossie. She preferred these days.

It had gradually become easier to leave him behind with Esther. In her first secretarial position she'd felt guilty for abandoning him with someone else all day, and sometimes fearful that Ossie might turn up and do something stupid when she wasn't there to stop him. Both of these feelings had gradually eased over time, but when she was out on her own, she still couldn't help but glance around her to check Ossie wasn't somewhere nearby, watching. Even if she tried to forget him, there was a reminder in the slight ache she still felt in her left foot with every step.

The ache was particularly bad this morning as she turned onto Selborne Avenue and made her way up the wide street. The pain reminded her of her last genuine attempt to alleviate Ossie's problems with a trip to the Victoria Falls: Selborne Avenue's grand buildings transformed into tall, stretching trees and its wide road collapsed in on itself to become a huge crevice in the earth. The Zambezi River flew out over the other side of the opening and thundered into the gushing crevice below. The air was aglow with a dancing mist that cooled the freckled skin on Muriel's arms and tickled her face. Up ahead, a faint fragment of rainbow shimmered in the mist.

Look Ossie, a watergaw.

Oh, he said flatly. He'd seemed cheery on the boat trip that morning along the orchid-flanked Zambezi; they'd spotted monkeys high up in the trees and waved cheerily at the native children playing on the banks. And now this dark turn.

They walked on in silence, Muriel veering closer and closer to the edge to get a better view of the drop. It was like the earth had proudly opened itself up for examination. The crevice wasn't a war wound, but rather a mouth gaping wide to tell its story, a great echoing chamber singing life itself.

Look at that. Isn't it just wonderful?

Hmm.

Don't you feel anything?

I'm sick, Muriel. You know I'm sick.

I thought this would help.

I'm tired. All this travelling.

Oh, but it was worth it. What a charming place.

Ossie took off his spectacles to wipe away the moisture that had accumulated across them. When he put them back on, he stared hard at Muriel. Without saying anything more, she calmly strolled away from the edge of the cliff and took a seat on a bench by a statue of Livingstone. She waited there until another couple came by. She got onto her feet and walked behind them, keeping a short distance of five or six steps. She listened carefully for the snap of twigs and the shuffle of leaves behind her. As they made their way back to the entrance to the Falls she decided she would leave Ossie for good.

Muriel arrived at Willoughby's Building on the corner of Selborne Avenue and Main Street. She worked here for an agency that dealt in insurance amongst other things she didn't quite care to fully understand. The agency's office was rented from

Willoughby's Consolidated which took up most of the ground floor. She loved the building with its teak doors and big brass handles, and the grassy central courtyard where she relaxed on her lunch breaks. Sometimes she'd even take her portable Remington typewriter out onto the large veranda on the first floor to type up some of her poems when business was quiet.

The owner of the business she worked for was a Mr Basil Frost. From the outset he'd been very keen to take her on and had cleared a desk for her directly across from his own. Even though he was nearer her father's age than hers, she quite enjoyed how he took an interest in her, especially when he asked to hear some of her poems. He was rather dishy with his thick moustache, deep-set eyes and finely cut suits. In some ways it was a shame he was already married, and in other ways she didn't mind this very much, knowing she wasn't in the mood for another husband anytime soon; it was just a pleasure to know that she was desired, and the sex in the office after hours hadn't been all that bad either.

I hope to see you at the dance tonight, Muriel? Basil said not long into her shift.

Perhaps, she said before allowing a small smile.

She piled up documents and files on her desk so that she could seclude some handwritten notes she'd taken in from home. Basil was too concerned with having a letch at her bosom to realise that she was spending her morning being paid by him to work on a redraft of a poem.

The poem was inspired by her time living in Gwelo, which she often missed. Ossie's last teaching contract had been at a small school amidst the farmland there; in this poem she wished to capture the town's slower pace of life where blacks and whites came together to work the land on more even terms than she'd experienced in Fort Victoria and Bulawayo, and where they'd lit paraffin lamps at night because of the lack of electricity, just like in her family's flat back in Edinburgh.

She'd felt far more at one with the natives of Gwelo, sharing meals with them as Sonny played with their children, no miner's wife in sight to pass judgement between drags of cheap Rhodesian cigarettes. But then life in Gwelo had taken a dark turn when Ossie had taken to firing off his Baby Browning pistol at home during their arguments. That's when she'd suggested their trip to the Victoria Falls.

On their return from the Falls, she somehow found a way to convince him that he should join the Rhodesian army to help with the war effort. As well as it being a way for him to disappear long enough for her to make plans to leave him, she felt sick at the thought of him torturing the children he taught. When he departed for the military camp, she hid his gun for the umpteenth time…

Muriel, would you care to have lunch with me? Basil was standing over her desk, his groin pressing up against the edge.

She'd been away in another dwam. She picked one of the documents off the pile in front of her and placed it down on top of her poetry notes.

You know, I would love to Basil, but I'm afraid I'm feeling rather bloated as a result of a breakfast crisis this morning. Hopefully I'll be back to myself for the dancing tonight.

Oh Muriel, you have nothing to worry about with a figure and a face like yours. You'll be the belle of the ball I'm sure.

Basil made his way out of the room and Muriel finally had peace to get back to her notes on the paraffin lamps, the vast maize fields and the kindness of the folk in Gwelo.

All the usual faces were in attendance at the Grand Hotel's Midnight Club that night: the Eisteddfod's secretary Ethel Davies; the eye specialist Dr Shankman through whom Muriel had met May; and, as always, one of the famous hotel owner Thomas Meikle's four daughters, a great lump of a woman who always seemed to be running these social events. Whenever she saw that Meikle woman, Muriel couldn't help but chuckle to herself at the irony of her family's Scottish surname, especially when Muriel caught sight of her tucking into the buffet.

As always, the bachelors in the room had swooped round May as soon as they entered the club, leaving Muriel a little outcast. Basil's wife had decided to come with him, so he gave Muriel nothing more than a smile and a wave from his table at the far end of the room. She made for the bar where Dr Shankman handed her a highball before she had a chance to order her own. After half an hour of struggling to hear each other over the band, and with their eyes nipping from the fug of cigarette smoke, they decided to take their drinks out into the hotel garden. They took a seat on an ornate cast-iron bench that had been painted to match the white magnolias all around the garden. The air was rich with the flowers' scent and the cloudless sky was packed full of stars.

Dr Shankman eventually asked about her divorce. As ever, she explained that her husband still wouldn't grant one – it was increasingly likely she'd have to say she'd deserted him. The solicitor had informed her that according to Roman Dutch Law, Ossie's mental instability was merely grounds for legal separation. Not divorce.

Shankman could clearly sense that he'd brought down the mood a little, so he asked Muriel if she would like to dance with him. She gulped down the last of her drink, stood up and put out her hand to the doctor.

Back inside the Midnight Club, all of the songs the band played transported her to a more innocent time in the dancehalls of Edinburgh: 'Let's Face the Music and Dance', 'Blue Moon', 'Nevertheless I'm in Love with You'... In Dr Shankman's arms she felt like she was eighteen again. To think that had only been five years before.

The ache in her left foot soon brought her back to reality. It worsened with each new dance and Dr Shankman's increasingly elaborate moves. As he spun her into his arms and held her from behind, she shivered slightly, remembering how Ossie had taken a hold of her that night he'd returned early from the military camp while Sonny slept in his cot. Ossie had come across the packed cases in the hallway and had flown into one of his episodes. He managed to find his gun taped under Muriel's side of the bed, all while she was writing a note for him at the kitchen table, completely unaware. Just as she'd got up to fetch more ink, he'd come up behind her and held the gun to her head. He asked where she was heading with the suitcases. For several long minutes, she tried to convince him to put the gun down. *Where the fuck do you think you're going?* he asked over and over as sweat ran down her face and her legs trembled.

Eventually, she couldn't take it anymore. She writhed out of his arms and tried to elbow and slap him away. There was a bang, quickly followed by a searing pain on the edge of her foot. She looked down at the pool of blood spreading across the kitchen floor. Her vision speckled and darkened. She fell to the ground.

Are you okay? Dr Shankman asked as he spun her away from him.

Oh, I'm absolutely fi–

A fist made contact with Dr Shankman's head and he was knocked sideways. Muriel screamed and the band quickly stopped playing. Ossie punched Dr Shankman again and he fell to the floor.

Ossie, stop it! she screamed. Stop!

Two men appeared and tried to hold Ossie back. He manically thrashed around like a snake and punched and kicked at the men, his spectacles flying off his face and smashing on the ground. Eventually they managed to drag him out through the doors.

After a long silence, Dr Shankman got up onto his feet, signalled to the band to start playing and then put his arms around Muriel's waist. She couldn't stop shaking as he moved her in time to the music. She dared to glance around the room. She caught

sight of that Meikle girl glowering at her – she knew
then that she was no longer welcome here.

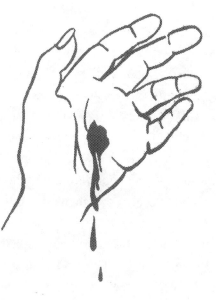

19th November 2016 – Bulawayo, Zimbabwe

The faceless woman impaled on the cross has large breasts and a jacket tied around her otherwise naked waist. Dark nails pierce her dark hands and one has been driven through both of her feet.

SACRIFICE
Clay
USD 700
Israel Israel

It's our last morning in Bulawayo and I've decided to visit the art gallery. On my way here, I passed by the long queues snaking out of banks until I came to the gallery's far quieter building. It's impressive with its wide veranda on the first floor and the large teak door at the entrance. I headed straight through to the courtyard café where I caught glimpses of artists at work in their studios while I sipped on my morning coffee.

It is known that Margaret would rather all of the paintings hung up in our Obs and Gynae department were put elsewhere. She says she likes clean, white clinical spaces, but I know the patients who have to wait around the place for hours on end think otherwise. I correctly guessed that the gallery would be one attraction she wouldn't want to join me in visiting. I needed this time on my own. I'm exhausted from the heat and all the listening. I'm not used to spending so much time with other people other than at Aberdeen Royal Infirmary.

Last night, the staff from Lady Rodwell were very kind and invited us out for a meal. I didn't expect it to be a Chinese restaurant, but I didn't complain given that the only local cuisine on offer at the Holiday Inn this week was deep-fried caterpillars. They were greasy and tough and eating them reminded me of when I used to chew on my shoelaces as a child. But who am I to judge? I grew up in Stonehaven, birthplace of the deep-fried Mars Bar.

The Chinese food was okay, and it was nice to see how the medical staff behaved together outside of the hospital. They seemed much more of a family than my colleagues back in Aberdeen. The younger doctors were still deferential to their seniors, but they spoke to them as though they were parents they admired and respected, especially the director. They all laughed heartily as he told us about his one and only visit to London where he'd got caught up in the drinking culture with some British doctors, woke up with a hangover that felt like death itself and vowed never to return.

I regretted ordering a Zambezi beer at that point and felt a little judged, although I was a little surprised that the doctors had all ordered regular Coca Colas – surely they knew that diabetes was skyrocketing in Africa? But then it wasn't exactly fading from Scotland.

The Zambezi did help me relax over time and I felt like I could be a little more myself and join in the conversation. Sisa and I got chatting about the fact we'd seen very little wildlife in the Matopos and I asked her and some of the other doctors at my end of the table how they felt about the game hunting business, especially after the furore over Cecil the lion.

Sisa burst out laughing.

Cecil?

One of the other doctors, Praise, rolled her big brown eyes.

Hunting has been going on without any news headlines for years, then someone from Oxford University writes an article and suddenly everybody's got a problem. She repeated, Oxford University, with her nose in the air and we all laughed.

The people out in Hwange, that is how they earn money to live, Sisa added. If they don't do this for tourists, they will be the dead ones.

But what if all the animals become extinct? I dared to ask.

Huh! You try staying completely still in a car while a hundred lions cross the highway at night and tell me they are going extinct, Praise said before laughing out loud. They were so close to us. My brother, ha! My brother had to hold me in my seat so I wouldn't try running out of the door.

We all laughed with her. I decided to ask nothing more about it to save upsetting the mood. The conversation soon turned to talk of marriage and, naturally, to my lack of a wife.

I move through to the next section of the gallery – it's filled with more contemporary work by local artists. There are some more sculptures and lots of abstract paintings that seem to be mainly of figures and faces. One painting, somewhat cartoonish in style, is of children linking arms and holding hands. The bright colours stand out on the black paper. There is another work by the same artist further along, this time a series of colourful numbers on black paper. The work is entitled CALL THE CREATOR.

Fighting my initial resistance, I take my mobile phone out, type in the +263 Zimbabwe dialling code and then enter the numbers in the painting. After a small delay there is a muffled ringing tone. I can feel my heart beating harder as it rings. Some part of me can't help but imagine that I'm actually calling god and that he or she might be up for answering some pressing questions I have. The ringing stops.

Yebo, sawubona?

2   99

…Hello?

Hello.

Are you… the creator?

…

I mean, do you paint? Are you an artist?

…

I look back at the square of paper next to the painting and read the artist's name.

Are you Daniel Kapadza? The artist of Call the Creator?

He laughs for a few seconds and I start to feel like I've fallen into some kind of trap.

You are in the gallery? he asks.

Yes.

Beautiful! Okay okay. Go to the window.

Even though I feel a little silly, I do as told and slowly walk over to the nearest window. It looks out onto the courtyard. No one is in the café or sitting out on the grass.

I can see you. Look up.

I do as told. In the doorway of one of the studios, a man with long dreads is waving at me. I see him laugh and, after a couple of seconds, I hear it through the phone.

Finally! Finally someone solved my puzzle! Wait there.

He hangs up and I watch him run across the balcony of the first floor studios and then down the spiral staircase next to the internal access to the main gallery.

I can't help but start fiddling with my shirt. I decide to untuck it and open another button at the collar. I straighten up my posture as I hear footsteps coming through the gallery.

Daniel? I say as he rushes towards me.

That's right!

He offers his hand. I slide mine across his and grip his thumb; he grips mine in return and we shake.

I'm Duncan. Nice to meet you.

Good to meet you too.

I like your painting, I say pointing to the one of the children playing. I like the colours. The way they pop on the black paper.

Ah, yes yes. It's one of my favourites. Do you want to know what it means? Daniel smiles in a knowing way even though I'm not sure what exactly it is he knows.

Sure.

Well, when we are children, we play with each other and we touch and we hold hands. Doesn't matter if you are a boy or are a girl. It is natural and we are happy. Then when we are older, people say that boys can only be with girls, and girls with boys. I think this is not natural. I think this is wrong.

I realise I am holding my breath as he speaks.

You're right, I say and exhale.

Yes. You understand. Where are you from?

Scotland.

Ah, beautiful! I would like to go there, he says. He looks back at the painting. Me and my wife, we have a meeting in our garden where teenagers who are gay can come and talk. A safe space. You know what I mean?

That's… that's amazing.

Yes. It's special.

We both stare at the picture in a silence that feels welcome and warm.

How long are you in Zim for? Daniel asks.

I leave tonight.

And we have only just met! That is sad.

I give him a little smile and then turn back to the painting.

Can I buy it?

Really?

Yes. I'd like to, I say getting out my wallet. I give him all the bigger notes I have left.

Thank you so much, Daniel says. He rests his hand on his stomach. I haven't eaten properly in two days. You have made my week!

You've made mine, I reply.

I sleep rough through most of the first short flight between Bulawayo and Jo'burg. I feel a little on edge as we wait in the long and chaotic queue to get through immigration at Jo'burg airport. Margaret and I have very little left to say to each other. I had imagined before we set off from Aberdeen that I would get to know her well, maybe even hear more about her sons and what she did in her spare time, but it has become apparent that she is always in professional mode.

Once we get through immigration and security, we wander off from each other in the shops. I try out most of the testers in the men's cosmetics department and then some of the free nibbles in the South African food shop. I'm a little taken aback when I see rugs made of real zebra hanging up outside the biggest gift shop. I think back to watching the zebras running wild and can't quite believe that it was just the day before. I suddenly feel a little cranky and decide to grab a coffee before I head to my gate.

On the plane, I'm seated in the middle between Margaret on the aisle and a middle-aged white woman with a dark bob and artificially plump red lips by the window. Before I get a chance to hunt out the headphones for the TV screen, the woman starts talking to me in a strong South African accent about how she is travelling to Paris for her makeup business and then onto China where her products are made. In between pauses, she purses her lips and stares over at a couple of black woman sat in front me and Margaret who are chatting away.

I wish they'd be a little quieter, she says before pursing her lips once more. And what do you do?

I'm a doctor. We're just heading back from Zimbabwe. We were visiting a hospital there. I point at Margaret but she is already fast asleep or pretending to be.

Oh, I see. I've never been. Some of my friends tell me it's still primitive there. Is it primitive?

My face burns and I don't know where to look.

What do you mean by primitive? I almost whisper.

You know, she says loudly. Primitive.

I don't know what you mean, but we had a great time. Everyone was lovely.

I finally find headphones in the seat pocket and begin trying to hunt out the socket to plug them into.

Oh yes, the woman says. Zimbabweans are lovely. They're great workers in my packaging factory in Jo'burg. They keep quiet and get on with the work, unlike the likes of her.

She points her finger at the black girl sat directly in front of me.

My South African workers are always so chatty and loud like *them*.

I snap.

I'm sorry, but the only person talking too loudly on this plane is you, so could you please shut the fuck up? I say quietly yet forcibly.

I shove the earphones over my head and select some music to drown out the woman's ensuing rant. My face is still burning as she pushes the call button above my head.

I keep my eyes fixed on my screen as a flight attendant arrives. I can see the pouty woman waving her hands out of the corner of my eyes. Her nail varnish is hot pink.

The flight attendant taps me on the shoulder and I remove my headphones. I turn and smile.

Yes, how can I help? I say.

The lady next to you insists on moving seat. I'm going to have to ask you to move out of the way for a second to let her out.

Of course. Of course, I say as I follow Margaret into the aisle.

The pouting woman takes her time collecting her things and getting out of her seat, and then another age to haul her case out of the overhead luggage bin.

When she finally disappears up the back of the plane, I slip back into our row and move right up into the window seat.

What was that all about? Margaret says in a daze.

Beats me, I reply.

I sit back and enjoy the view from outside the window. After we take off, I think of home and sleepily watch as shooting stars slide across the darkness.

20th November 1943 – Salisbury, Southern Rhodesia

Ye must forsake yer dear husband,
Yer little young son also,
Wi me tae sail the raging seas,
Where the stormy winds do blow.

Muriel cut the ballad short when she remembered it didn't end well. She was definitely being tempted to cross the seas by a daemon, but she supposed hers was Socratic in nature rather than supernatural. And oh… to see the sea again.

Her suitcase was already full. She had to swap some items to make room for those possessions she couldn't bear to leave behind. She supposed her work clothes wouldn't be as essential for now: she removed a couple of smart blouses and a pair of small black heels to make room for her Bible, the references from her employers back in Bulawayo and her writing award certificates. The latter had been her saviour: she'd used them to convince Mr Smith, the magistrate who'd officiated her marriage, to sign a permit allowing her to study literature and drama in Cape Town. From there she'd make her way back to Britain, whatever it took.

She wasn't fazed by the prospect of travelling closer to the heart of the war for the war had already come to her. She'd met the most charming man from the Air Force, Arthur Foggo, who'd been tall and fair-skinned like the Afrikaans boy on the *Windsor Castle* all those years ago. Just when she'd thought she'd given up on affairs with men, he'd come along. But as soon as a little part of her had begun to soften for him, he'd been posted home.

She unfolded the telegram he'd wired to her after he'd arrived at Cape Town. It was stamped 6 – 10 – 42.

Leaving immediately, will write you as soon as I arrive,

Love Arthur Foggo

Around the same time she'd received the wire that night, his ship had been torpedoed in the waters just outside of Cape Town. She no longer wept at the sight of the square of paper. Over the past year, Arthur had become another loss amongst a sea of many. She'd pretty much lost everything except her Mind.

The hardest parting had been saying goodbye to Sonny just days before. She packed the wee bunny he'd played with as a baby in her suitcase. Unlike her son, it would be able to cross the sea in wartime. Even if Sonny were allowed to travel with her, Ossie would be able exert his legal rights to the child from within the confines of the mental hospital in Gwelo where he'd recently ended up.

And if she stayed any longer, this country would kill her: she packed a box of aspirin in her case, the remnants of all that had been offered to her when she'd fallen ill with septicaemia near the end of her time in Bulawayo. She'd suffered from bouts of illness ever since. In order to live, and to seek out any kind of life at all, she had no option but to send Sonny to board at a convent school in Gwelo, but she knew one day soon she'd be reunited with him.

She was sure she'd also be reunited with May who'd gifted her a pair of pearl earrings before risking her own voyage back to Britain at the start of the year, soon after discovering her husband had been killed in the war. Muriel put the earrings on, fearing that if she attempted to pack them, they'd be lost through one of the holes in the case that had burst open during her move from Bulawayo.

She clasped the case shut and looked over at the pile of books she hadn't been able to squeeze in. She couldn't care less about leaving behind her weighty copy of *The South and East African Year Book*; it had proved of little use as a guide over the past six years. It was far harder to leave behind her translations of Kierkegaard's journals she'd picked up from Philpott and Collins back in Bulawayo, but she supposed she would maybe be able to read other copies of them at the library in Edinburgh, and most definitely in London, her ultimate destination. As for the few remaining books she'd been able to get her hands on, she'd reread them so often that they resided within her; there was no need for physical copies.

She fiddled with her wedding ring, now on her right hand, and wondered whether she should leave it behind. She decided to hold onto it – she might need to pawn it to get by in the city if finding a job was problematic or if the war took a turn for the worse.

Once everything was packed away and tidied in the flat, she locked it up and posted the keys in the mailbox in the stairwell. She walked in the growing morning light from Fountain Court down through the long avenues of jacarandas to Salisbury train station, only stopping now and then to switch her heavy suitcase between her hands. In amongst the trees, grey louries called out to her, *Go-away... go-away... go-away...*

I am for Christ's sake! Muriel cried. I am.

Outside the station, she was taken aback at the sight of someone standing by the door waiting for her. Esther's face glowed so beautifully in the morning light that Muriel was moved to tears.

Oh, I'll miss you so much. Thank you for everything. I couldn't have *lived* without you.

I hope I will see you again one day, Esther said.

I hope so too, Muriel cried as she hugged her goodbye.

They never would see one another again: twenty-two years later, dazed from the longest flight of her life thus far, the only person Muriel would come across from her days in Southern Rhodesia would be a small English woman with skin that had dried and cracked with the sun. The woman would ask, Do you remember me?, but Muriel would fail to recall her. You don't remember me… I'm Tootsie Bailey, the woman would say, and she'd take Muriel's hand and it would all come streaming back: the way they'd held hands on their morning walks during her first years in Southern Rhodesia. Tootsie, her one and only confidante at that time, and she'd almost forgotten her. Ossie had been right when he'd turned to her after one of his episodes and said, *One day this will all be like a bad dream to you.*

Alone, Muriel made her way through the train station entrance with her heavy suitcase. To think she'd come all this way to Rhodesia for a man to take nearly everything from her. But there was one thing she'd taken from S.O.S. that she would never give back.

Name, madam? the ticket officer asked at the desk in the train station.

Muriel, she replied. Muriel Spark.

Printed in the United States
By Bookmasters